With special thanks to Tabitha Jones

For Connor Michael Chivers and Ryder Blake Gilbert

www.seaquestbooks.co.uk

ORCHARD BOOKS

First published in Great Britain in 2016 by The Watts Publishing Group

1 3 5 7 9 10 8 6 4 2

Text © 2016 Beast Quest Limited.
Cover and inside illustrations by Artful Doodlers with special thanks to Bob and Justin
© Orchard Books 2016

Series created by Beast Quest Limited, London

The moral rights of the author and illustrator have been asserted.

A CIP catalogue record for this book is available from the British Library.

ISBN 978 1 40834 072 1

Printed and bound by CPI Group (UK) Ltd, Croydon, CR0 4YY

The paper and board used in this book are made from wood
from responsible sources.

Orchard Books is an imprint of Hachette Children's Group
and published by The Watts Publishing Group Limited,
an Hachette UK company.

www.hachette.co.uk

REPTA
THE SPIKED BRUTE

BY ADAM BLADE

ORCHARD

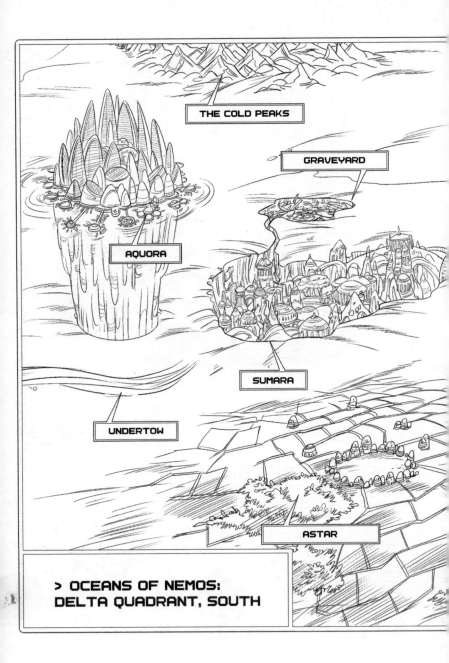

GUSTADOS

VERDULA

FIELDS OF FLOWERING KELP

>SCIENTIFIC REPORT TO GENERAL ZAN

LOCATION: FORTRESS PRIME

GENERAL, OUR TANKBOT ARMY IS READY
FOR ACTIVATION! ALL WE NEED NOW IS
THE POWER TO CONTROL IT...

WE HAVE PICKED UP THE SIGNAL OF THE
SUPERCOMPUTER NEARBY, HEADING TOWARDS
A PRIMITIVE NATIVE SETTLEMENT. SOON
IT WILL BE WITHIN OUR GRASP — THE
MOST POWERFUL AI EVER KNOWN, WHICH
STEERED OUR ANCESTORS TO THIS PLANET.
IMAGINE SUCH A MIND COMMANDING A
THOUSAND OF OUR DEADLY TANKBOTS!

FORTRESS PRIME WILL BE UNSTOPPABLE,
AND THIS NEW OCEAN WILL BE OURS.

ALL HAIL GENERAL ZAN!

STORY 1:

FORTRESS PRIME

CHAPTER ONE

BREATHER ALERT

Lia shot past Max's watershield, her webbed hands clasped tight around her swordfish's dorsal fin and her sliver hair rippling behind her. A trail of glittering bubbles streamed from Spike's tail as he and Lia swooped ahead, darting through bright shafts of sunlight slanting down from the ocean surface.

"Left behind, Max!" Rivet barked from the passenger seat. The dogbot's nose was almost pressed against the watershield.

"I don't think so, Riv!" Max said. He slammed his foot down hard on the escape pod's accelerator, whooping at the sudden burst of speed. A moment later, he drew alongside Lia and Spike.

Lia turned and grinned. "Not far to go now!" she said, her voice reaching Max through his headset.

Max glanced at his navigation screen. They'd travelled almost ten leagues from Lia's home city, the Merryn capital, Sumara. A cluster of green dots on the screen marked the location of a small underwater settlement just ahead.

"You are going to love Astar!" Lia said. "The Flowering Fields of Kelp are amazing."

"Holiday, Max!" Rivet barked.

"Sounds great," Max said. The words came out kind of flat, but Lia didn't seem to notice.

Her eyes shone with excitement as she leaned over Spike's back, racing into the current. Max sighed. *Flowers...* He didn't want to hurt Lia's feelings, but seriously? Flowers? Still, with open water all around them, what better chance to find out what his new modified space pod could do? Excitement tingled down Max's spine. He jerked the steering lever. *Here we go!* The pod spun over in a barrel roll. Max's stomach flipped and bright bubbles whipped past the watershield.

"Dizzy, Max!" Rivet barked.

"Sorry, Riv!" Max said, pulling out of the roll. "But you have to admit, my new pod is awesome!"

Lia looked back over her shoulder and raised an eyebrow. "It isn't bad for a bit of tech. But you didn't actually make it, did you?" she said.

Max shrugged. "Maybe not, but without

my TLC, this beauty would still be rusting at the bottom of the ocean." He ran his gaze over the blinking lights and displays that covered the curved, black dashboard, nodding with satisfaction. He'd salvaged the escape pod from the wreck of the SS *Liberty* – one of the spaceships that had originally brought human life to Nemos. "Not that it was actually rusting, of course," he added. "The hull's pretty much indestructible. And with my mods, it's got to be the fastest vessel under the sea. But that's nothing compared to the on-board computer! Iris, increase space thrusters!"

The small green holographic face of a human girl flickered into life before him, projected from a silver capsule attached to the dashboard. The SS *Liberty's* AI computer interface – Iris.

The hologram flashed Max a grin. "No

problem, Max!" she said. "Just wait for this…"

The thrusters roared. Max felt the vibration deep in his chest as his body was mashed back into his seat. The seascape around him melted into a blur of blue and white. Max yanked the steering lever, flipping the vessel upside down.

"Wahoo!" he cried.

At his side, Rivet whimpered. "Too fast,

Max!" the dogbot barked.

Max gave the steering lever one last twist, then righted the craft, letting it slow so Lia and Spike could catch up. "It's okay, Riv," Max said. "Iris'll look after us."

Lia frowned as she arrived at his side. "I still don't think it's such a brilliant idea trusting your life to space tech," she said. "What if Iris goes crazy again?" Rivet shuffled back in his seat, away from Iris's image.

Max laughed. "Don't worry, Riv," he said. "Iris is fine now I've repaired her damaged circuits." He glanced down at the AI's smiling face. It was hard to think that only recently she'd been trying to wipe out all intelligent life on Nemos. Since Max had fixed her software, she wouldn't hurt a barnacle. "You know what, Iris?" Max said, "I'm starting to wonder how I ever got by without you."

Iris beamed. "Thank you, Max!" she said. "I

feel the same way. The company in Aquora is so much better than on the SS *Liberty*."

Outside the sub, Lia cleared her throat noisily. "If you're quite done chatting with that computer, you might want to check out the view. We're almost there."

Max peered into the deep blue water ahead to see dark humps of rock structures on the seabed, surrounded by green and brown fields of billowing seagrass.

"That's Astar?" Max said. His villainous half-robotic cousin Siborg had grown up there. Max didn't know what he'd been expecting, but it certainly wasn't a few stone huts surrounded by weed. He could see maybe fifty beehive-shaped dwellings, arranged around a central clearing. A few larger buildings scattered the outlying fields, but there was nothing remotely like the glittering coral towers of Sumara.

"It's a rural farming community," Lia said. "Actually, you might want to cut your engines. We don't want to frighten anyone – they won't have seen a sub before. And the only Breather they've met is Siborg – hardly a good advert for your species."

Max killed the thrusters, letting the pod drift slowly out over the fields.

Soft sunshine filtered through the clear water, casting dappled shadows over the

greens and browns of the seagrass. Max could see Merryn of all ages working alongside each other, dressed in simple green tunics, their long hair gathered back in cornrow braids. The older Merryn rode swordfish, cutting the fronds of grass with long scythes. Children followed behind, bundling the cut crops into wagons pulled by sleek black and white orcas. The sound of their voices and laughter drifted up to Max on the current.

"Let's head down and say hello," Lia said. She and Spike dipped towards the field. But at the same moment, a bloodcurdling scream cut through the ocean.

"Mummy! A monster!"

Lia and Spike froze. Max scanned the field below to see a small girl pointing up at his sub, her eyes wide with fear. A plump, rosy-cheeked woman bundled the child behind her and lifted her scythe, scowling darkly up at Max's sub.

"Who dares bring Breather tech here?" a gruff voice shouted. An ancient, wrinkled Merryn man swooped up out of the field on the back of a swordfish, waving a coral staff. He stopped before Max and Lia. A dozen muscled farmers swarmed to his sides, brandishing what looked like crystal-tipped scythes and pitchforks.

"Sharp sticks, Max," Rivet barked.

Max turned to Lia and groaned. "Can't we even take a simple sightseeing trip without someone wanting to kill me?"

Lia rolled her eyes. "Leave this to me." She held up her hand to the sea-folk before her. "Don't be alarmed," she called, "Max is with me. He's a friend to the Merryn people."

The old Merryn scowled, his rheumy eyes

filled with scorn. "Don't be daft, lass," he said. "You'll be telling me next you've made friends with wolf-sharks. Get out of the way and let us deal with the Breather scum." The farmers around him drew closer together, their crystal-edged weapons gleaming.

Lia hitched her chin and shook back her hair. "I've never been a stickler for titles," she said, "but I'd prefer 'Your Highness' to 'lass'. I'm Princess Lia of Sumara, and Max is my friend."

The old man let out a bark of laughter. "Princess, is it? You must think we were born yesterday." He turned to the farmers behind him, and lifted his fist. "Round 'em up, lads!" he cried.

Max quirked an eyebrow at Lia through his watershield. "That went well, then," he muttered.

Lia scowled back at him, then lifted her

spear and turned it on the approaching men.

"I order you to stop in the name of King Salinus!" she shouted. But the farmers surged onwards, waving their makeshift weapons.

Here we go again! Max thought, gripping the pod's steering lever. "Too late for that, Lia," he said. "Let's get out of here!" He revved the pod's engines and zoomed up, away from the seagrass field, leaving the angry farmers behind. In his rear viewer, he could see the old wrinkled Merryn waving his scythe, his pale eyes bulging with rage.

"Watch out, Max!" Iris cried.

Max glanced ahead. *Whoa!* Two sturdy Merryn with glinting knives and furious frowns swooped towards him, riding swordfish. Max tugged the steering lever and dived between them, leaving the Merryn farmers spinning in his current. *Too easy!*

"Max!" Rivet barked, "Grumpy farmers

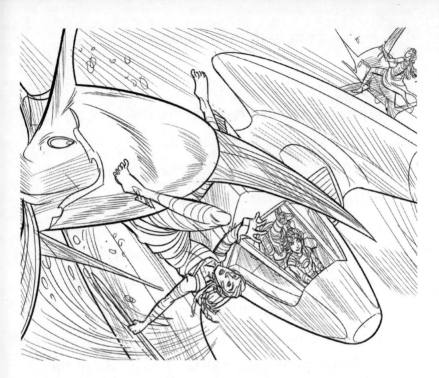

got Lia!" Max glanced in his rear viewer. His stomach sank. Lia and Spike were right where he'd left them, surrounded by Merryn jabbing at them with farm tools. Lia's spear flashed out, again and again, blocking the villagers' blows, but already her movements were slowing and her face was pink with effort. Max slammed his sub around and angled it towards her, just as a huge Merryn built like an Aquoran amphibio-tank swung a club at her back.

"Lia! Look out behind!" Max cried. Lia turned, blocking the club with the shaft of her spear, but the force of the blow sent her flying from Spike's back. She tumbled through the water and disappeared into the seagrass. The villagers swarmed after her, their eyes flashing with victory.

"Lia hurt!" Rivet barked.

"Shall I shoot?" Iris asked.

Max swallowed, horror building inside him as more villagers piled towards Lia. Spike swam above the mob, clicking in dismay. "We can't blast away a bunch of farmers – even if they are acting like thugs," he said.

"Of course not!" Iris said. "But if I lower the power we can give them a shock."

Max nodded. "Do it!" He aimed his blasters into the field, near to the knot of farmers, and fired. A bright ball of energy fizzed through the water. *BOOM!* The shockwave rippled outwards through the seagrass. A cloud of dirt and tattered weed mushroomed up, sending villagers and swordfish tumbling.

"That should show them we mean business," Iris said. Silt and fronds of vegetation filled Max's view. Frightened shouts echoed around him. Max stared into the clearing water, trying to catch sight of Lia. When he finally spotted her, his chest tightened. She stood, pale-faced and wide-eyed, in the grip of the huge farmer. The sharp edge of his scythe was pressed against her throat. The man glared up at Max's sub.

"Get out of that evil Breather vehicle," the farmer shouted. "Now. Or I'll put an end to your treacherous Merryn friend!" The man gave Lia a sharp shake and Max saw her flinch. Anger boiled inside him, but he swallowed it down and scrambled into

the sub's rear airlock. He swam out slowly,
keeping his hands in full view.

"That's better!" the farmer said. "And you'd
better not try any evil Breather tricks!" He
turned to the men all around him. "Gag and
bind the prisoners! It's time to take them to
the village hall for sentencing!"

Perfect! Max thought. *We're being arrested.
And I thought this holiday would be dull…*

CHAPTER TWO

SIBORG'S LEGACY

Max seethed with fury, his hands tied tightly behind him and a seaweed gag biting the corners of his mouth. A weather-beaten Merryn with leathery skin held his shoulder, pushing him through the chest-high seagrass. Ahead, the muscled farmer still had his scythe at Lia's throat. Max glanced behind him to check on Rivet and Spike. Rivet gazed back at him mournfully, tied to the back of an orca.

"Don't worry, Riv," Max mouthed. *We'll sort this out, I promise.* Spike swam silently, sandwiched between two swordfish twice his size. Max could just make out the space pod behind them, a pair of cow-eyed manatees nosing it along.

The seagrass finally thinned. Max and Lia were pushed through the last fronds, in among the cluster of beehive-shaped huts that passed for a village. Wide eyes watched them from the darkness of stone doorways and feral-looking dogfish flitted out of their path. Up close, Max could see the dwellings were made from wedges of stone, piled together with no mortar between the bricks and no windows – just a single door with a thick lintel.

Before long, the procession reached a larger building at the edge of the central clearing. Max was tugged to a stop before a low stone doorway, then shoved inside behind Lia. Without his hands to help him swim, he sprawled clumsily into the room. He heard an angry growl, and glanced back to see Rivet being dragged inside, along with Spike and the pod.

The chamber was roughly circular, with driftwood benches arranged around the edge, packed with flinty-eyed Merryn. Small glowing points on the walls cast a milky light into the gloom. Peering closer, Max could see the light came from glowing anemones. At the far side of the room, a stout woman sat straight-backed in a wooden chair, flanked by a pair of female guards holding coral spears. The guards' tunics shone with plates of crystal armour. Beads decorated their cornrow braids, and long coral knifes hung from their belts. They stared ahead, as still as statues.

The woman in the chair wore a long green gown embroidered with swirling lines

and flowers. Her russet hair flowed loose around her broad, handsome face, and deep expression lines scored the skin around her stern, dark eyes. A coral sword, edged with shimmering crystal, rested across her lap.

The aged farmer that had captured Max and Lia swam to the centre of the room and bowed his head before the woman. "Chief Elra," he said, "this girl led a Breather with dangerous tech to our village."

Elra's stern gaze flicked from Max and Lia to the Merryn farmers holding them. "Remove the prisoners' bonds," she said in a low, resonant voice. "It is time to hear their defence."

Rough fingers fumbled at the back of Max's head, and his gag was tugged away. A moment later, his hands were free. He flexed his shoulders and rubbed his wrists. As soon as Lia's bonds were removed she stepped towards Elra, her face flushed with fury.

"Surely you must recognise me!" Lia said. "I've seen you at councils in Sumara. I'm Princess Lia. If this is the way you treat all visitors, you need a lesson in hospitality!"

Max saw Elra's eyes widen and the colour drain from her cheeks. "Princess Lia!" she said, "Of course I recognise you now your gag is removed! You have my sincerest apologies. My people don't visit Sumara often, and…

well…you must admit, your choice of companion…is somewhat alarming."

"Max is my friend," Lia said. "I brought him here to show him the Fields of Flowering Kelp, and he wanted to take a look at the place where his cousin grew up."

Elra's hands flew to her mouth. "That boy is the half-Breather's cousin?" Max heard gasps of horror from the Merryn seated all around him. Elra shook her head firmly. "I really do have to object, Your Majesty. Astar is a sacred village. After what happened with Simon, there really is no place for Breathers and their tech here." Murmurs of agreement whispered around the room.

Max's anger flared. Siborg might be evil, but he hadn't been born that way, and he was still Max's cousin. He stepped to Lia's side, his fists clenched. "Maybe if you had shown Siborg some kindness after his father abandoned him, instead of treating him like a freak, he wouldn't have lost the plot like he did. Did you ever think of that?"

Elra's colour darkened and her eyes flashed. She opened her mouth to speak.

"Look," Lia cut in, "Max has saved the Merryn people from danger more times than I can count. My father has given him freedom of the realm. You have no right to turn him away."

Elra closed her eyes, and took a deep breath. After a moment, she opened them again, and managed a smile. "Your Majesty. This has taken us by surprise. If the Breather is your friend, of course he must stay and tour our village. However, I will send guards to join you once you reach the flowering kelp. It is, after all, sacred to my people."

Lia shrugged. "If that makes you feel safer," she said, "but they'd better be a bit less heavy-handed than your farmers." Lia rubbed at a thin red line on her throat, and Max saw Elra blanch again.

"Of course," Elra said. "They will treat you with honour."

Lia turned to Max with a grin. "In that case, let's go!" She beckoned Spike from the side of the room, and leapt up onto his back.

Max stared at her in disbelief. "You still want to go and look at some flowers after all that?" he said.

"Of course!" Lia said.

Max rolled his eyes. "Okay, fine," he said. "But I choose our next holiday destination!" He glanced around the room. Rivet lay with his nose on his paws, three guards with pitchforks standing over him. The pod was pushed up against the wall by the door. "Come on, Riv!" Max said, crossing to the pod. He opened the airlock, and swam in.

Rivet bounded away from his guards and scrambled in behind him. Once they were seated, Max spun the pod around.

Lia and Spike were waiting by the door. As Max manoeuvred the pod after them, every pair of eyes in the room turned to follow.

"Oh, for goodness' sake!" Max growled. "You'd think I had three heads. Iris, let's get out of here. This had better be worth it!"

Iris activated the thrusters and the pod zoomed after Lia. They swooped up over the huts of the village and out into open farmland. Waves of seagrass swept past beneath them, stretching into the darker blueness ahead. Low stone walls broke the fields into plots. The occasional rocky outcrop or domed storage building poked up from the seabed, but other than that, there was nothing but rippling grass. It seemed to go on for ever.

Finally, Max saw something surprising in

the deep blue water ahead. It almost looked like the tree line of a forest. As they drew closer, the shadowy shapes became clearer, and Max gasped in wonder. A twisted mat of thick, winding green trunks rose up from the seabed, separating into tangled branches. Each branch was tipped with a cluster of bright blossoms shaped like butterflies.

Sunset reds and oranges fluttered in the current alongside pearly pinks and blues.

"Wow!" Max breathed. "I thought it would just be a field of flowers. This is more like an underwater jungle!"

"Pretty flowers, Max!" Rivet barked.

Lia turned to Max and grinned. "I knew even a tech-head like you would be impressed.

It's all one plant, connected by the roots. It's more than three thousand years old, and the trunks are almost indestructible."

"Then it's been on Nemos longer than humans have!" Max said.

"That's right," Lia said. "And, like Elra said, it's sacred to the Astarians. Leave the pod here. They don't like tech in the kelp fields."

"I'll look after the pod," Iris piped up from the dashboard. "I want to gather info on the seagrass crops for my data banks, anyway."

"Thanks, Iris," Max said. He opened the airlock at the back of the craft and climbed out, followed by Rivet. Iris turned the pod around and shot away, back towards Astar.

"Let's go and explore!" Lia said. She and Spike slipped between the twisted kelp trunks into shadow. Max followed with Rivet at his side. Beneath the kelp canopy, everything was quiet, with just the gentlest current making the flowers overhead sway, casting dappled green light all around them. Max swam between the thick, twisted trunks, peering into the gloom. The ocean floor was hidden beneath a deep mat of tangled roots, and winding greenery crowded in on every side. Something about the stillness and quiet set Max's nerves on edge. He realised he was holding his breath and let it out slowly.

"This place is kind of eerie!" he whispered.

Lia nodded. "It's almost like the plant knows we're here…"

"Danger, Max!" Rivet barked, shattering the quiet. Max jumped, his heart thundering. Lia jolted upright on Spike's back. Max followed the line of Rivet's gaze. Something was blocking out the light ahead, plunging the forest into darkness – something vast and black and swollen, hovering over the canopy. And it was coming straight towards them.

CHAPTER THREE

MYSTERY FROM OUTER SPACE

"Let's take a look from above," Max said, gripping his blaster. Lia nodded, her eyes on the strange black shape blotting out the light. Max kicked upwards through the twisted branches of kelp with Rivet at his heels. Lia and Spike swam beside him. Together, they pushed through the bright flowers and peered out over the canopy. *Whoa!* The object was a huge black oval, about the size of a battle cruiser. It was drifting slowly through the water towards them. Max couldn't see any propellers or fins – the object's surface was completely matt-black, like the shell of a giant egg. Max frowned. *It doesn't look like a Robobeast…*

"Let's move closer," Max said. "But be ready. There could be something inside it."

Rivet bared his teeth, and let out a low growl. "Ready, Max!" he barked. Spike lifted his sword and gave a sharp click.

They all swam slowly towards the vast, bulging object.

"What could it be?" Lia asked.

"I don't know," Max said, "but I don't much like the look of it. Rivet, run a scan. We don't want any nasty surprises."

Rivet's eyes flashed red, and he stared hard at the oval shape. Then he shook his head. "Metal too thick, Max," the dogbot barked.

"What is this thing you have brought here?"

A sharp voice spoke out behind them. Max spun to see Elra's two female guards riding glossy orcas, their coral spears pointed at his chest. *They must have followed us!*

Lia scowled. "So much for treating us with honour!" she said. "We didn't bring that thing. But I'd say you're lucky we're visiting. It could be dangerous. We need to check it out."

The guards looked at each other for a long moment then turned back to Max and Lia. The taller of the two gave a nod. "As you wish, Princess. But first we need to get it away from the kelp," she said. "And away from the people," the other added. "We'll take it to one of our empty seaweed stores. They are far enough from town that there should be no danger. You can take a look at it there."

Max, Rivet, Lia on Spike, and the two guards riding their orcas, lined up behind the metal object, and started to swim, pushing it slowly through the water over the flowering kelp. Max kicked his legs hard behind him, surprised they could manage to shift the gigantic object at all. Whatever metal it was made from had to be very light.

Before long, they reached the rippling fields of seagrass. The farmers stopped work to watch them, hands on hips and eyes narrowed with suspicion. Finally, Max spotted the humped shape of a huge stone seaweed store near the edge of the field.

One of the guards dived down and opened the large driftwood doors to the store, then returned to help Max and Lia push the metal object towards the building, and angle it through the wide entrance.

Once the massive black egg was settled on the floor, the guards bowed to Lia. "We'll leave you to your investigations, Your Majesty,"

one woman said, her eyes flicking nervously to the black metal ovoid. "If you need us, just call." Then they spun and quickly swam away.

"Right," Max said, glancing around the room. The stone walls were scattered with more anemones, giving off a soft white glow. The floor was smooth, clean sand. Apart from the piles of seaweed and the monstrous metal egg reaching almost from wall to wall, the room was empty. "Not quite up to Aquoran lab standards, but it will have to do."

Max swam all the way around the object looking for any dents or markings, but it was completely uniform. Something about the black metal was strangely familiar, though. Max ran his hand over its cool, smooth exterior, then rapped it with his knuckles, making it ring with the deep note of a gong. Spike darted back from the object, clicking nervously. "Noisy, Max!" Rivet barked. Lia frowned.

"Don't do that again!" she said. "That thing gives me the creeps. If there's some spooky space creature inside, we don't want to wake it up!"

Lia's words sparked a memory. "Of course!" Max said. "That's why the metal seems familiar. There's some of it on my pod, and on the SS *Liberty*. It's from outer space!"

"Perfect!" Lia said. "I thought I was joking! So, you're telling me there really might be an alien inside?"

"More likely this thing was left over from the human colonisation of Nemos, two thousand years ago," Max said. He pressed

a button on his watch. "Iris, come and find me. I want you to look at something."

Max squeezed past the black object until he reached the doorway. The pod was swooping towards him over the field. It slammed to a stop at his feet. There was a click, and the airlock to the pod swung open. Max climbed inside, waiting for the water to drain away before entering the cockpit. He plucked Iris's pod from the dashboard, teasing its small metal legs from their sockets, then swam back into the store.

"Iris, can you tell me what this object is?" Max asked, holding the silver capsule that contained Iris's circuits before the smooth metal shape. The water above the capsule flickered, and a hologram of Iris's face appeared, her brow furrowed in a puzzled frown.

"I don't know what it is," Iris said, "but

I know what it's made from. Targonite. It doesn't exist naturally on Nemos, though. The colony ships had to bring ingots with them."

Lia frowned. "If that egg thing dates from the colonisation, why has it only just appeared?"

Max shrugged. "Maybe it's been made more recently, from metal salvaged from the wrecks?"

Rivet let out a sudden snarl, and leapt away from the black egg. The vast metal shape shuddered. Max jumped back, grabbing his blaster as the object transformed in a blur of movement. Thick black plates flipped up all along the top of the egg, folding back on each other, creating an armoured shell of scales. Clunks and clanks echoed off the stone walls as massive spikes thrust from holes in the shell in all directions. The shape

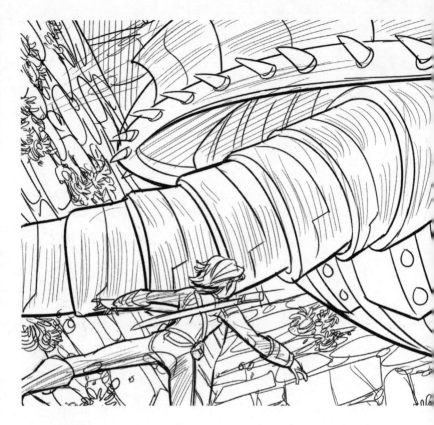

jolted upwards, and four broad flippers with sharp claws telescoped out from holes in the base. The flipper nearest Max bore a single word, etched in big block letters. *REPTA*.

Max's whole body sunk with dread as he read the name. "It's a Robobeast!" he shouted, staggering back. He gazed up to see a colossal head shoot out, broad and

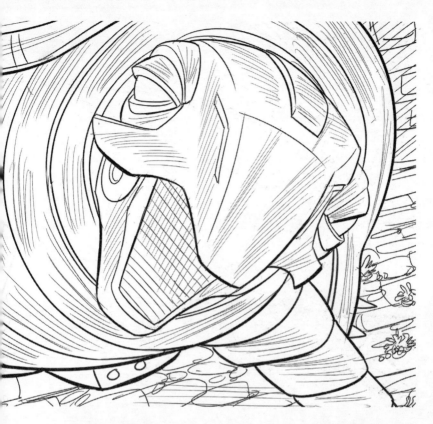

scaly, tapering to a sharp, beak-like nose.
Two yellow eyes, glowing like molten rock,
flicked about the room. *A robotic turtle!* The
turtle's head turned suddenly towards Max,
and lunged, its extendable neck whipping
out ferociously. The beak flipped wide open,
ready to crunch Max to pieces.

CHAPTER FOUR

THE SPIKED BRUTE ATTACKS

Max dived sideways, flinging his body away from the crushing metal jaws. "Get out of here!" he cried, his legs and arms thrashing though the water as he scrambled for the door. Lia swooped ahead of him on Spike, with Rivet just behind.

They bundled out into the field, and turned. Through the open door, Max saw all the spines covering Repta's body suddenly shoot outwards on metal chains.

"Get back!" he yelled, scrambling away as fast as he could. *BOOM!* The vast metal spines punched through the stone brickwork of the seaweed store, sending chunks of rock hurtling in all directions. The building collapsed in a cloud of billowing silt. Max crouched low to the seabed, his arms

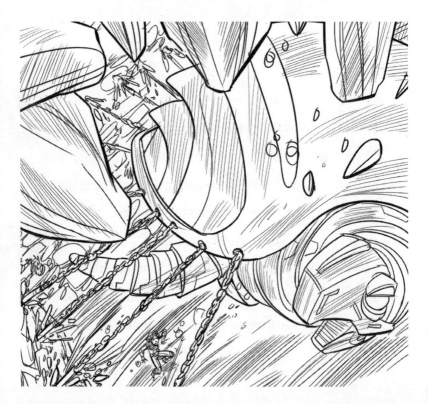

thrown over his head. Choking grit churned around him and stones pummelled his body. Through the din of falling rock, he could hear Rivet barking frantically. *I hope he's all right. And Lia and Spike.*

When the water finally cleared, Max scrambled up to see Repta rising up above the rubble of the store, its fiery eyes scanning the scene. Max stared in horrified awe. Where did that thing come from, and why?

"Lia? You okay?" Max called into his headset.

"Heading back your way, Max!" Lia replied. "We were swept into the field by the blast!"

Max lifted his blaster, aiming it at the giant Robobeast. Spines and cannons and pincers covered its Targonite shell and its glowing eyes gazed back at him. Max swallowed. His blaster had never felt so inadequate... *Here goes!* He fired. The energy beam sliced through the water and bounced off Repta's shell without leaving a mark.

"The weapon's ineffective," Iris said, speaking urgently from her capsule still clasped in Max's hand. "You need to escape!"

Max nodded. But where to? He glanced around to see nothing but seagrass and shattered rock all the way to the kelp tree line in the distance. And he couldn't lead the Robobeast towards the village...

"Turtle coming, Max!" Rivet barked. Max looked up to see Repta's massive, armoured head shoot out on its long, stretchy neck, snaking straight towards him, metal jaws gaping.

Max kicked his legs and pumped his arms, thrusting himself away from the robot's powerful jaws. They slammed shut on empty water with a clang. Repta's long neck recoiled back towards its shell, snatching its jaws away. "Riv, I need a ride!" Max cried, his heart hammering. He gripped his dogbot's back. At the same moment Repta flicked its gigantic flippers and surged towards them, a colossal weight of bristling metal and cruel chomping jaws.

Rivet's turbos roared as he tugged Max up and out of range of the robot's snapping beak, then sped over a field of seagrass. Max glanced back to see the giant turtle shoot after them, its powerful legs a blur of movement. It swooped low over the fields behind them, gaining on them fast. Astarian farmers shouted and dived out of the way of the mountainous metal creature, throwing themselves face down into the field.

"I'm coming, Max!" Lia cried. She was bent low over Spike's back, riding fast towards Repta, her spear drawn back.

Repta's long neck curved round at the

sound of her voice, eyes narrowing. "Watch out, Lia, it's spotted you!" Max cried.

A thick spine shot out from Repta's shell straight towards Lia and Spike, dragging a thick chain behind it. Max's heart clenched at the sight of the sharp point surging towards his friends. Spike swerved out of the way just in time, and Max shuddered with relief. *BAM!* The spike smashed into a Merryn

grain store with a force that chilled Max to the bone. Repta didn't slow, powering on after Max and Rivet, dragging the metal point from the building, tearing chunks of wall away with it. The building heaved and collapsed, grey rubble hurtling outwards. Over his shoulder, Max caught a glimpse of Spike dodging flying stones before he and Lia were engulfed in the cloud of silt and rubble. *I hope they're okay,* Max thought. He wished he could go and check, but Repta's eyes were focused back on Max, sharp beak inching closer, giant flippers ploughing through the sea.

"We have to get out of range," Iris said from her capsule, still clasped tight in Max's fist.

"Trying, Max!" Rivet barked. His turbos whined as he angled upwards and climbed through the water, away from the Robobeast. Max kicked his own legs to add power. Rivet turned hard left, so sharply Max's stomach flipped, but Repta kept as close as if they were connected by an invisible chain, its glowing eyes fixed on Max. With a hum and a clank, a pair of fat, black blaster cannons thrust out on either side of Repta's massive head. *Zap!* A stream of red energy balls fizzed towards Max and Rivet. "Rivet! Dive!" Max cried. Rivet dipped his nose and powered towards the seabed, dragging Max behind him like a kite tail. Max let out breath of relief as the energy balls sailed above them. Rivet levelled and raced onwards over the field, the seagrass a blur beneath them.

BOOM! An energy ball ploughed into the ground ahead. A fountain of mud erupted from the field and a shockwave surged through the water. Max braced himself. The current hit, ripping Max's hands from Rivet's back. Rivet shot away ahead of him, then turned, his red eyes scanning the water.

"Over here, Riv!" Max called, righting himself in the silty water and swimming as fast as he could towards his dogbot.

"Danger, Max!" Rivet barked, his eyes flashing bright with alarm. Max glanced behind him to see the massive, dark shape of Repta blocking his view. A metal spine attached to a chain shot from the creature's side, straight towards his chest, opening into a three-pronged claw.

A bolt of terror seared through Max's veins. "Argh!" Strong pincers clamped around his chest on either side, crushing his ribs. *It's got me!* Max tried to squirm free, but Repta's claw jerked back suddenly, tugging him through the water so fast he couldn't breathe.

The metal chain retracted until Max found himself dangling right before Repta's huge eyes. Max twisted, trying to free himself, but the claw clamped tighter, the points digging

into his flesh. "Lia! Where are you? Help!" Max cried.

"On my way, Max!" Lia said.

"Coming, Max!" Rivet barked. But their voices seemed far away, and Max couldn't turn to look for his friends.

His heart thundered against his ribs as Repta stared back at him. Then another grappling spike shot from the robot's armoured shell.

"No!" Lia screamed, her voice filled with anguish. Max watched the deadly spike racing towards him, and swallowed hard. *This is it. It's over. I'm going to be skewered!*

CHAPTER FIVE

BORDER CONTROL

Max threw up his arms, the three-pronged claw filling his field of vision. He heard Lia gasp, and closed his eyes, waiting for the pain. There was a click, and he opened his lids a crack to see the tips of Repta's claw clamped round Iris's capsule in his hand.

"Let go of me!" Iris shrieked. Then the capsule was gone, torn from Max's grasp by the claw. Max felt the pincers clenched about his chest tighten painfully. He was dragged sideways through the ocean, then flung free. He pumped his arms and legs, trying to slow himself as he tumbled towards a pile of broken stone that had once been a store.

Thud! Max's back slammed into the rubble. *Crack!* His head snapped back against jagged rock. "Ow!" Max clutched his head. Through the black spots swimming before his eyes, he saw Repta swoop in a U-turn then power away through the water, Iris's capsule clamped tight in its claw. The hologram of her terrified face formed in the water.

"Help, Max!" she cried, before her image was snatched away.

"Max! Are you okay?" Lia asked, arriving at his side and leaping from Spike's back. Rivet appeared beside her, his silicone tongue slathering Max's face.

Max pushed Rivet away and shook his throbbing head to clear his vision. He put a hand to the back of his skull and winced as he touched an egg-sized bruise. "I'm fine," Max said, cold dread stealing over him. "But Repta stole Iris!"

"Bad turtle escaping!" Rivet barked.

"Not if I can help it," Max said. "Iris is my friend." Lia offered him her hand. Max took it and clambered up. "And there's also the small issue of her being a supercomputer with the processing power to destroy the planet," he said.

Lia nodded. "Repta will be taking her straight back to its maker."

Max glanced at the metal turtle, speeding away from them, its vast feet churning though the ocean. "But who could that be?" Max said. "Siborg's locked up in Aquora, the Professor's been swallowed. The only other person on Nemos with the know-how to create Robobeasts is Iris, and she could hardly steal herself. And, anyway, she's good now." Max spotted his pod lying half-buried under the remains of the seaweed store Repta had emerged from. He kicked up from the seabed. "Let's go," he said. "We might be able to catch Repta up if we go at full speed."

"We have to try," Lia said.

Max slipped through the airlock into the pod, followed by Rivet. He gunned the engines, angling the craft up and out of the rocky debris, leaving a trail of silt behind him. Spike and Lia swooped to his side. Ahead, Max could still make out the distant form of Repta, a dark blot against the shimmering surface above.

Max and Lia rocketed through the ocean, speeding above the seagrass fields after the giant robot. Terrified Merryn swam for their lives as Repta passed overhead, before the creature swam away into the open ocean.

Max and Lia followed at full speed, gaining fast on the Robobeast's bulky form. Before long, Max found himself grinning.

"Nothing can outrun us now, Riv," Max said, the pod zooming after Repta as the robotic turtle crested a rise in the ocean floor. The view opened up before them, and Max's smile froze. He slammed on the pod's brakes, a surge of terror squeezing the breath from his lungs. Through his headset, he heard Lia gasp.

A huge, green dome hovered just below the surface of the ocean ahead, stretching right across their field of vision. The transparent structure rested on a circular metal platform, and Repta was paddling towards it, dwarfed by the green bubble above. The whole thing seemed to be slipping away from them, as if motorised.

Through the shimmering bottle-green side

of the dome, Max thought he could make out the towers and spires of a city skyline – not far off the size of Aquora but under the water, sealed within a force field, like a scene in an Arctirian snow globe.

"What is it?" Lia asked.

Max touched his viewing screen with two fingers, zooming in on the structure ahead.

Now Max could see rows of bullet-shaped skyscrapers, magnified and distorted by the curved green force field. Sleek hovercrafts zipped between the buildings, and green lights glowed in the windows. "It looks like some sort of underwater city," Max said. He recognised the matt-black metal that surrounded the base of the dome. "That bottom bit's made of Targonite," he said, pointing, "which means it's either come from outer space, or it's made from metal from the colony ships."

"But what does it want with Iris?" Lia asked, her voice edged with worry.

Max shrugged, and tightened his grip on the pod's controls. "Only one way to find out. Come on. Let's take a closer look!" Max revved the pod's engines and zoomed after Repta. The robotic turtle was slowing on approach to the underwater city, angling towards the near edge of the metal base of the dome. As Max drew closer to the strange transparent shield, he noticed scores of silver spheres zipping around it, orbiting the underwater city. Repta sailed past one of the whizzing balls and the silver sphere stopped dead in its orbit. A lens flicked open at its centre, like an eye. A beam of light shot from the eye, and scanned over Repta's shell, before blinking out.

"Those things must be some sort of border patrol," Max said. "Something tells me we should avoid getting spotted. Stay close. I'll plot a course." Lia nodded. They edged towards the city, flitting between the silver patrol-bots' orbits. "There are so many," muttered Max, concentrating hard. He craned forwards in his seat, tracking the dizzying movement of the orbs, while Lia and Spike stuck close to the pod's tailfin. Max held his breath each time he dived past one of the metal robots, and only let it out when he saw Lia and Spike were safe.

Closer to the dome, the orbiting patrol-bots began to thin out. Max risked a glimpse at the city beyond the force field, causing his jaw to drop in wonder. A central carriageway led between rings of sleekly tapering high-rise buildings, heading towards a circular stadium at its heart. Flags billowing from poles surrounded the amphitheatre, and the pale beams of floodlights angled down towards the centre. The way the flags moved looked strange, until Max realised they were fluttering in air. *The city must have its own atmosphere.* Max spotted movement and glanced down to street level. "People," Max said in awe. "Hundreds of them." The dense mass of figures were all moving towards the amphitheatre, arranged in ranks.

"It looks like an army," whispered Lia through his headset.

Anxiety squirmed in Max's belly. Up close, the city looked like a military base.

A patrol-bot whizzed past and Max swerved. At the same moment, light glared through Max's watershield. "Halt!" a robotic voice demanded. *We've been spotted!* thought

Max with a jolt of panic, hitting the brakes. Lia and Spike came to a sharp stop beside him in the blinding beam from above. "Analysing!" the robotic voice blared. The light flashed like a strobe, making the cockpit flicker, then suddenly, it blinked out. Max squinted up to see a silver patrol-bot directly above, its glassy eye wide, and the tip of a fat blaster cannon poking from the pupil at its centre.

CHAPTER SIX

UNDERCOVER AGENTS

Max grabbed the control stick, ready to zoom away, but then released his grip. *If we try to escape we'll be shot for sure…but we can't just sit here!* Before he could make up his mind what to do, the glass eye closed over.

"Domestic technology, with human inhabitant and animal life detected," the automated voice blurted. "Proceed." Max wiped a film of sweat from his head. *Phew!*

"It must think the pod is from inside the

city because it's made from Targonite," Lia said.

Max grinned. "Which makes you animal life," he said. Lia rolled her eyes.

"Max! Look!" Rivet barked. Repta was fast approaching the domed city. A wide door in the platform at the base slid open before the giant Robobeast.

"Quick, Lia!" Max shouted. "Get into my slipstream." Max angled the craft towards the door and gunned the engines. He glanced back to see Lia and Spike right behind him. Ahead, Repta was disappearing through the opening. As soon as the robot was inside, the door started to close. *We'll never make it!* Max slammed his turbos to full speed.

The sudden force threw him back in his seat. Rivet whimpered. The edges of Max's vision blurred and the dashboard rattled. Max could feel the flesh of his cheeks being tugged backwards from his face... But the closing door was just ahead... *Yes!* The pod shot through into brightly lit turquoise water and Max slammed on the brakes. He glanced back to see Lia and Spike hurtling straight towards him. Spike angled his body, skidding to a stop, and Lia flew from his back. Max winced as she struck his watershield and bounced off, then righted herself in the water. She was grinning from ear to ear. "Whoa!" she said. "That was quite a ride!" She looked about, taking in their surroundings. Max did the same.

They were in a circular docking pool lined with metal tiles. But it was empty. "Turtle gone!" Rivet barked.

"He can't have gone far," Max said. "Let's head up and see where we are." He steered the pod upwards, with Lia and Spike at his side. They broke through the water's surface into a round chamber with matt-black walls lined with pipes. Lia sniffed the air and wrinkled her nose. "It stinks of engine oil in here!" Fluorescent tubes in the ceiling cast a sickly glow over everything, and Max could hear the quiet hum of pumps. All around the edge of the pool, sleek black aqua bikes floated in docking stations, and green uniforms hung on pegs alongside black deep suits. Black boots were lined up beneath the uniforms. There were no people or robots in sight.

"Nice bikes!" Max said, admiring their slim, simple frames. "I wouldn't mind a ride on one of those."

Max steered the pod towards the far end of the pool and scrambled through the airlock. Lia was already climbing from the pool, leaving Spike watching from the water. As she turned, Max was surprised to see her

familiar face surrounded by long wet hair. Then he realised why. Normally on land, her features were hidden behind her Amphibio mask, but since her gills had been changed by the seaweed of the primeval sea, she could breathe air.

Max heaved himself out of the pool beside

her. "It's going to take me a while to get used to seeing you out of the water without your mask," he said.

"I don't know if I'll ever get used to it," Lia said, brushing her fingers over the gills at her neck. "Breathing air feels weird!"

"It looks weird too," Max said, frowning. He pointed to the green uniforms and peaked caps hanging from the walls. "We'd better cover you up."

"Charming!" Lia said.

Max grinned. "Just so you fit in."

Lia scowled, but she reached for a jacket and tugged it on, pulling the collar up to cover her gills. She picked out a pair of boots and wiggled her webbed feet into them. Then she bundled her silver hair on top of her head and tucked it under a cap.

Max ran his eyes over her webbed hands and frowned. "If you keep your hands in your pockets, you might just about pass for human, as long as no one looks too closely." Max pulled on another of the green uniforms over his damp wetsuit.

"Now, which door?" Max asked, scanning the room. There were three to choose from – great slabs of metal set in frames, each facing in a different direction.

"How about the one with the massive robotic footprints leading up to it?" Lia suggested. Max looked around the edge of the pool. Big shallow puddles led from the water's edge to the central door.

"You may be on to something," he said. He turned to Rivet. "Riv, stay here with Spike and guard the sub. There aren't any dogbot uniforms, I'm afraid." Rivet's ears sagged, but he plunged back into the pool and paddled to Spike's side. Spike's silver eyes were fixed gloomily on Lia.

Lia leaned over and patted his sword. "I'll be back before you know it," she said. Then she turned to Max and nodded.

"Time to find out what a moving

underwater city is like inside," Max said. "Follow those prints!"

CHAPTER SEVEN
GENERAL ZAN

Max and Lia followed Repta's wet footprints, until they stood before the smooth grey door leading out of the docking room. Max spotted a circular pad marked EXIT on the wall. He swallowed, trying to shift the metallic tang of anxiety and excitement in his mouth, then pressed the pad. The door slid silently open. Max glanced at Lia, and she smiled nervously back at him from under her cap.

"Let's go, then!" she said. Together, they

stepped from the docking room.

The door shut behind them, stranding them in a concrete plaza busy with people dressed in drab green uniforms, all marching in the same direction. Max and Lia pressed themselves back against the door. Everything they could see was bathed in a sickly green light filtering down from the dome above. A huge metal statue on a pedestal dominated the plaza, forcing the marching people below to flow around it. The figure was tall and broad, with powerful muscles bulging beneath the folds of a military uniform. His stern eyes gazed fixedly into the distance from under a peaked military cap, and his hand was raised in salute. Etched on a plaque riveted to the pedestal Max read the words: GENERAL ZAN.

"He looks fun!" Lia whispered.

"Yeah, fun like a dose of the gill pox,"

Max said.

Beyond the statue, steep steps climbed to the foot of a bridge that swept across the city between the bullet-shaped high-rises. Hoverbikes and hovercars with smoked glass windscreens and shiny, insect-like armour zoomed past above, headed in the same direction as the people – over the bridge, towards the open-air amphitheatre on the far side. The regular puddles of Repta's steps, now scuffed by boot prints, led onto the bridge.

"Hurry!" Max heard one man mutter as he marched past. "The rally is about to begin!" The man spoke standard Aquoran with a faintly clipped, old-fashioned accent.

Max met Lia's gaze and tipped his head towards the bridge.

"Shall we?" he said. Lia nodded. They crossed the plaza together, slipping into pace with the trooping crowd.

The steady flow of marching feet made the bridge wobble and sway, but the crowd pressed forwards around Max. He and Lia kept close, their heads down, Lia's hands shoved firmly into her jacket pockets. When they reached the far end of the bridge, the curved walls of the amphitheatre rose up before them. Long flights of stairs reached from the walls in all directions, like the points of a star. The citizens on the bridge broke into lines, marching single file towards the many flights of stairs. Max and Lia joined the line for the nearest staircase, nipping in behind a young woman with a braid of long black hair reaching down her back from under her cap.

They filed to the top of the stairs and found themselves on a precarious, narrow walkway. Tiers of benches dropped away beneath them, interspersed with flights of steps leading to an open space below. The seats were quickly filling with green-clad citizens, pressed shoulder to shoulder, all facing the space at the centre of the amphitheatre. Max's eyes were drawn there too. At his side, Lia gasped. The arena was filled with hundreds of black robots, lined up in ranks. Each was about the size of a human lying belly down. Plates of armour covered their bodies forming a dome, almost like the shell of a turtle, and each had four flippers and a sharp-beaked head.

"It's an army of mini Reptas!" Lia said.

Max nodded. "But they don't look like they're activated." The robots were completely still. Their heads, attached to long, snaking necks, rested on the ground, and their eyes were dark.

"He's not deactivated, though," Lia said, pointing. At the head of the robot army, to the right of where Max and Lia stood, the tiered seating came to a stop, and a semi-circular platform jutted out from the amphitheatre wall. Near the back of the platform stood Repta. The giant turtle's head swung from side to side as he surveyed the ranks before

him. The sight sent a chill down Max's spine.

"We'd better take a seat before someone spots us," Max said. They picked their way down the nearest staircase, and perched at the end of a bench. From all round them, Max could hear the coughs and shuffles of a thousand people, waiting. Then a roar of engines from above broke the quiet. A huge cheer went up from the crowd and the uniformed watchers all stood as one, their hands raised in identical military salutes. A sleek hoverbike zoomed overhead and came to a stop above the platform where Repta waited. The passenger on the bike leapt neatly down, and strode to the centre of the platform to a deafening chorus of cheers.

The man was tall and powerfully built, his muscular chest and broad shoulders emphasised by silver tassels at the shoulders of his military jacket. His head was covered with a peaked cap in the same gun-metal grey as his suit. Beneath the cap, fierce grey eyes gazed out at the crowd, set deep above a sharp, chiselled nose, and a firm, square jaw covered with stubble. Max recognised the man – his narrow lips were pressed into the same grim line as the statue at the head of the bridge. General Zan!

The general held up his hand, and the crowd in the stadium fell silent.

"Welcome, people of Fortress Prime!" the general said, his strong voice filling the stadium.

"Hail, General Zan!" the crowd replied in a solemn monotone.

"We have spent many years searching for the lost spaceship, the SS *Liberty*," the general continued, pacing the stage as he spoke. "The vessel brought our ancestors to Nemos two thousand years ago. We knew our mother ship held a computer powerful enough to control the robot army we have built." The general gestured to the inactive machines ranked below him. "A feat which no other computer could achieve. At times, our quest seemed fruitless." General Zan stopped pacing and paused for a moment, scanning the crowd, every citizen watching him with a zeal that set Max on edge. The general suddenly lifted his fist. "But then there was hope!" he cried. "We picked up a distress call from the *Liberty*, and followed it here to this distant quadrant. And now, thanks to Repta the Spiked Brute, we have recovered what we were hunting." Max's stomach churned with dread as the general opened his balled fist, revealing Iris's silver capsule. "Behold, the supercomputer!"

A tremendous cheer erupted from the crowd, so loud and long Max thought it might never end.

When the cheer finally died away, the general continued. "This computer is powerful enough to command our tankbot army. With these weapons, we will force every city in Nemos to submit. We will rule over them.

We will take command of their resources. The empire of Fortress Prime will grow!"

Another cheer started, but died suddenly as Iris's face projected from the capsule in the general's hand, glowing above the platform.

"No!" Iris cried, her face scrunched up with fury. "My friends are coming to rescue me! I will never obey you!"

The general's stern smile didn't falter. He slid his free hand into the pocket of his jacket and removed something small and shiny, like a metal caterpillar. "Oh, I think you will," he said. "This is a control worm." The general pressed the metal sliver against Iris's capsule. "No, no, no!" she cried, her eyes wide with alarm. The small silver object flickered, and was gone, burrowing inside the capsule. Max's mouth and throat went dry. Iris's face twisted in agony, shimmering in and out of sight. Then Iris's hologram flickered from green to red, and her anguished expression settled into a blank, steely stare. "I obey only Fortress Prime!" Iris cried.

"No!" Max gasped softly. "That worm must be interfering with her systems!"

General Zan crossed the stage with Iris's face projected before him, his boots clicking on the stone. He stopped beside

Repta and fixed Iris's capsule onto the back of the giant turtle's head. The metal legs fused into the turtle's shell.

Repta's eyes blinked into life, shining suddenly with a bright red light. A broad grin spread across Iris's face, which was still projecting from the capsule. "Awaken, my army!" she commanded, her voice echoing from speakers embedded in Repta's shell.

An electric hum spread across the floor of the amphitheatre. The eyes of every tankbot blinked on, the same red as Repta's. Their long necks extended, and their heads came up to stare at the glowing image of Iris.

Max felt hot and sick. "Iris is evil again," he said, his voice little more than a croak.

Lia nodded. "And now she's in charge of an army of attack robots. Not to mention one of the deadliest Robobeasts we've ever faced!"

STORY 2:

ATTACK ON ASTAR

CHAPTER ONE

A DESPERATE CHASE

Max stared at Iris's blood-red image hovering in the air above Repta, an evil grin still plastered across his childlike face. Then he glanced at the ranks of armoured tankbots, waiting for her command. *I have to stop this. Now!*

"Lia!" Max hissed, "I need to get Iris away from Repta – can you create a diversion?"

Lia ran her eyes over the amphitheatre full of uniformed people and glowing-eyed tankbots, then glanced at the platform. Her lips twitched into a smile as she watched General Zan pacing, still ranting on about the power and virtue of Fortress Prime. "I think I can manage that," Lia said. "But I'll need your blaster." Max handed it over, and Lia tucked it into her belt.

"Good luck," Max said.

Together, they slipped from their seats and started off at a crouching run down the steps, past tiers of closely packed men and women. Not a single head turned their way. Every watcher sat straight-backed and silent, their eyes lit with a dreadful fervour as they stared at General Zan.

Once Max and Lia reached the arena, they skirted around the tankbot army, towards a narrow staircase that jutted from the stage. Max couldn't help noticing just how many robots there were, and how sharp the spikes covering their thick armour looked.

General Zan's voice echoed loudly around them as Lia scampered up the steps and onto the front of the stage. Murmurs spread through the audience near to Lia, and people pointed towards her. She turned to face the crowd. Max watched as she pulled off her cap and shook out her long silver hair, then held up her webbed hands.

"Hello, ladies and gentlemen," Lia shouted, her high voice cutting through the general's monologue. "Merryn princess here!"

Gasps of horror and wonder went up from the crowd. General Zan's head snapped around.

"Someone remove that…creature this instant!" General Zan demanded, pointing at Lia, his eyes flashing with fury.

Nice one, Lia! Max thought. He crouched low and hurried across the atrium to a second flight of stairs that led to the far side of the stage where Repta waited. Anxious murmurs and shuffling footsteps echoed through the arena behind him as he climbed. Suddenly, the throb of engines cut through the air, and a hoverbike zoomed overhead. Two guards leapt from the bike and darted across the stage towards Lia, snatching blasters from their belts. Lia grinned and lifted Max's pistol, sending a red energy beam towards the dome above. Then she lowered her arm and aimed right at General Zan's heart. "One more step, and I'll shoot!" she said, gazing steadily at the guards. Both men froze, their eyes flicking from Lia to General Zan, who stood still, his jaw clenched with rage.

Max seized his chance. He darted onto the stage and slipped behind Repta, then gripped hold of a protruding spike and vaulted up onto the robot's black, armoured shell. He scrambled over the slippery metal, digging his fingers and toes into the joints between the plates. Around him, the air was thrumming with tension, all eyes on Lia and General Zan. Max could hear his pulse loud in his ears. The back of Iris's red, holographic head hung in the air before him. Below it, her

capsule glinted in the green light from above. Max grabbed the capsule and tugged it free, glancing towards the tankbots in the arena. To his relief, every single pair of glowing eyes blinked out. *Now for a swift exit!*

"Let me go!" Iris screeched from his hand. General Zan's head whipped around, despite Lia's blaster still pointed at his chest.

"Stop him!" the general boomed.

Repta's neck craned back over its shoulder, and its eyes, glowing yellow again, fixed on Max. The metal shell beneath Max bucked. He bent his knees, and went with the movement, leaping from Repta's back into the air, just as the Robobeast's crushing beak snapped out. The beak slammed shut with a clang, but Max landed on the platform and careered onwards, towards the guards watching Lia. He lifted his legs and launched a flying dropkick at the side of the nearest guard.

"Oof!" The man lurched into his partner. "Ow!" Both stumbled and fell.

"Cover me, Lia!" Max cried, scrambling past the fallen guards towards their hoverbike, which was still idling at the edge of the stage.

Lia fired her blaster, zapping the ground at General Zan's feet and peppering the stage around the guards as they tried to clamber up. Cries of alarm erupted all over the arena, along with the sound of booted, running feet. Max leapt onto the guards' hoverbike, opened the throttle and shot towards Lia. The general lunged at him, his face purple with rage and his eyes blazing, but Max swerved and slammed to a stop beside Lia. She leapt onto the bike behind him. Max revved the engines to full.

The bike shot forwards so fast that Lia let out a yelp. Max tugged back on the steering lever, feeling Lia's arms tighten around his waist as they zoomed over the stadium. Energy bullets whizzed past from the stage, and cries filled the air. Max angled the bike upwards and sailed over the stadium wall towards the bridge that spanned the city. From behind, he could already hear sirens and the throb of hoverbike engines. He glanced back to see the flashing green lights of emergency vehicles speeding towards him. He surged on, leaning

low to streamline their flight.

Zap! A blue energy bolt shot past, vanishing with a flash as it slammed into the curved green force field in the distance. *Zap! Zap!* In his wing mirror Max could see more energy blasts fizzing towards them. He veered sharply away from the bridge, zooming between two black high-rise towers. "You'll never escape Fortress Prime!" Iris cried from the capsule

in Max's hand. Max shoved it into his pocket and swerved left, then right, swooping between the buildings. The blaring sirens and flashing lights behind him flared and faded as he slalomed between skyscrapers, but energy fire still ricocheted off the black buildings either side. Lia's arms squeezed Max's ribs so hard he could barely breathe.

At last, the end of the bridge was in sight, along with the cargo dock where Max knew Spike and Rivet waited, guarding the pod.

Max sent the bike into a steep dive towards the cargo door. "Lia! Blast the door!" Max cried. Lia's arm released his waist. *Zap!* Her energy blast sailed ahead of them and slammed into the door. "Good shot, Lia!" The door slid open. Max swooped inside and hit the brakes.

"Max!" Rivet barked, jumping to his feet and wagging his tail. Spike lifted his sword from the water and clicked a greeting. The sirens were getting louder by the moment.

"Rivet, get in the pod," Max shouted. He and Lia leapt from the bike. Lia threw off her jacket and dived into the pool beside Spike. Max scanned the cluttered walls and spotted the controls for the sea door. He flicked the "Open" switch, then ran for his pod. The sound of sirens blared in his ears and the flash of green lights filled the room. *They're here!*

Max dived into the water and climbed through the sub's airlock into his seat beside Rivet, and hit the engines.

Vroom! The sub shot through the open sea-door and into the ocean. Lia was already speeding away from the city on Spike. But just as Max thought they had escaped, he saw something which made him gasp A patrol-bot was spinning towards Lia, a blaster poking from the centre of its single open eye.

CHAPTER TWO

ULTIMATUM

"Lia! Watch out!" Max cried. He saw Lia's head snap around, and her eyes widen as she registered the patrol-bot whizzing towards her. Spike flicked his tail, diving sideways as Max aimed his blasters at the spherical robot, and fired. Red beams knifed through the ocean, hitting the patrol-bot dead centre. The silvery orb exploded in a flare of light, sending out a starburst of twisted metal and blackened wires.

"Thank you, Max!" Lia's voice came

through the pod's speakers.

"More eye bots, Max!" Rivet barked. Max scanned the water ahead to see two more spherical robots zipping towards them from either side, one above and one below. White spotlights shot from their open eyes, casting long beams through the water. Lia and Spike swooped between the beams. Max followed close behind them. *Whoa!* The cockpit lit up white, a shaft of light hitting it from above. Max twisted the steering lever, swerving right, but the beam seemed to be locked on the pod. Max's pulse raced. *I'm right in its gun sights!* The thought gave him an idea. He twisted his steering lever, spinning the pod around and angling upwards until the beam was right in his eyes.

"Blinded, Max," whined Rivet, from the co-pilot's seat. Max couldn't see a thing either, but he had to be facing the robot's open eye.

He felt for the trigger for the sub's torpedoes. *Fire!* He held his breath…

BOOM! The light in the pod flared even brighter, and Max tensed. *Am I hit?* But then the light flickered out, and a rain of metal debris pattered against his watershield. *Phew!* Max blinked to adjust his eyes to the gloom, straightened his steering, and sped on. The ocean around him looked clear, with only Lia on Spike ahead. He glanced back to see the green bubble dome of Fortress Prime with its orbiting patrol-bots shrinking into the distance.

"Escaped, Max!" Rivet barked.

"Only just, Riv!" Max said, bringing the pod parallel to Lia and Spike. "Now all we have to do is work out how to fix Iris." He tugged her capsule from his pocket. Iris's face projected out, blocking his view.

"All enemies of Fortress Prime must be

destroyed, foolish Aquoran!" Iris shouted, her red eyes glaring. Max stuffed her capsule back in his pocket so he could see through the watershield.

"I would say fixing her is a high priority," Lia said. "But how? I take it we can't turn her off and on again?"

"We can't turn her off without destroying her," Max said. "And even if I wanted to do that, I don't know how. No. We need to get rid of the control worm. But to do that, I need time to think and somewhere to work."

"You will never succeed," Iris's muffled voice shouted from Max's pocket, her red image distorted as it emerged from his pocket.

"Oh, give it a rest!" Max said. He flipped a cover in the dashboard open, and pulled out a screen-cleaning wipe.

"Never!" Iris boomed. "You will be—" Max smothered the screen wipe over the capsule, killing her projection.

"Hey! Unmask me!" Iris's muffled voice went on. "I command you in the name of General Zan!"

Max sighed. Beyond the watershield, Lia shook her head.

"No off button was definitely an oversight in her design," she said. "We should head back to Astar, and quickly. We need to warn them about Fortress Prime so they can evacuate. You can work on Iris, and I'll send a message to my father and your people in Aquora, telling them to gather a force."

"Good plan," Max said.

They surged onwards at full speed. Before long, Max spotted the vivid colours of the Flowering Fields of Kelp ahead. They passed over the bright kelp and the cannon-blasted seagrass, then dived towards the village. From above, the damage caused by Repta was all too clear. Several of the dome-shaped buildings were little more than piles of rubble, and chunks of masonry littered the fields. Max spotted the green-gowned form of Elra in the clearing at the heart of the village. She was pointing, and calling orders to the villagers, who were collecting scattered stones and piling them into carts.

Max and Lia made straight for the Astarian leader. She looked up, her eyes narrowing to angry slits as she spotted them, and her hand went to the hilt of her coral sword. "Why do you return after all you've done?" she cried. "The Breather brought a tech monster to our village. He is not welcome here!"

"No!" Lia said urgently. "That robot attacked Max. It wasn't his fault. And now the people who sent the Robobeast are coming this way. They mean to destroy us all. You have to evacuate the village and

head to Sumara for safety."

Elra and all the Merryn surrounding her froze. They stared up at Lia and Max in silence, their eyes wide with terror.

"You have to believe me!" Lia said, her hair billowing around her as if caught by a sudden current. Max felt his pod shift forwards, nudged by the same shift in the ocean's waters. Then he noticed that Elra and her people weren't looking at Lia. They were looking at something behind her. Max turned, and his heart jolted. The huge dome of Fortress Prime was edging silently towards them, casing a vast shadow over the seagrass fields below it.

"What is that thing?" Elra asked.

"Bubble city, Max!" Rivet barked.

Max gritted his teeth. "How did it get here so fast?"

"There's no time to evacuate now!" Lia said. "What should we do?" But before Max could come up with a plan, a wide door in the metal base of the city slid open, and a familiar robotic form shot out.

"Repta!" Max cried. The snapping turtle's thick armour plates bristled with spikes, and two huge cannons jutted out on either side of its reptilian head.

With a sudden hiss of static, General Zan's voice echoed all around them. "Give us the computer now, or this primitive settlement will be destroyed!"

Max and Lia exchanged a horrified look through the pod's watershield.

"Please!" Elra begged from behind them. "You must do as they say. You can't let them destroy Astar!"

Max swallowed hard and turned his sub to face Elra and her people. "But I can't hand Iris over either," he said. "If I do, General Zan will have the power to destroy all of Nemos, starting with Astar."

Elra clenched her jaw and drew herself up tall, her nostrils flaring and her eyes ablaze. She lifted her coral sword. "In that case, we will have to fight!"

CHAPTER THREE

COUNTDOWN TO DESTRUCTION

"You have five seconds, and counting!" Zan's voice boomed through the ocean. Max spun his sub back again to see Repta's broad, clawed feet push through the water, propelling the massive Robobeast over the seagrass fields of Astar until it hovered almost above the village.

"Five…" Zan cried.

"Evacuate the village!" Lia told Elra. "Get all your people as far away as you can!"

"Four…"

Max aimed his torpedoes at the huge robotic beast while Elra shouted orders. Merryn swam for their lives around him, grabbing makeshift weapons, children and possessions, fleeing for the fields.

"Three…"

On Spike's back, Lia lifted her spear. Max shot her a look of grim determination through his watershield.

"Two…"

Elra swam to Lia's side, her russet hair billowing, the hilt of her long coral sword gripped in her webbed hand. Merryn farmers swarmed to join her. Max recognised the old man who had met them on their arrival, a fierce light in his pale eyes and a crystal-tipped pitchfork in his hand. The strong Merryn man who'd held Lia at knifepoint now had his scythe raised high to defend his village.

"One!" Repta's cannons fired together, shooting twin energy beams at a settlement, which exploded. With a loud blast, Repta followed it with a hail of energy balls which plunged towards the village.

Max gulped as he spotted one sizzling straight towards them. "Look out!" Max

cried, swooping the pod upwards. Beneath him, Lia, Elra and the other Merryn scattered, their legs and arms a blur.

BOOM! An energy blast smashed into a stone Merryn home, blowing it apart. *THUD!* Another building exploded into rubble. Jets of bubbles, dust and flying debris obscured Max's watershield.

Max spun his sub around and got Repta in his sights, but a group of Merryn farmers were attacking the robot with their scythes and pitchforks, their weapons bouncing harmlessly off the robot's metal hull. *I can't fire and risk hurting them!* A grappling spike exploded from the robot's side, shooting past the farmers. The hook shot past Max's sub and plunged into a building below. Repta snatched the spike back, breaking the stone dwelling apart, hurling debris all over Astar.

At the same moment, the turtle's blasters

fired, sending a pair of sparking energy orbs smashing into the village hall. Everywhere Max looked there was chaos, churning water and flying debris. He could hear stones clattering against his sub. Silt billowed around him. Merryn clinging to swordfish and farm tools swirled past, caught up in the current from the blasts.

"Max! Look out to your left!" Lia's voice shouted through his headset. Max turned to see a huge spike on the end of a thick metal chain hurtling towards his pod. Before he could move, the sub jolted horribly, and a metallic crunch filled his ears. *We've been hit!* Max was thrown sideways in his seat as the pod jerked, tugged by the thick chain towards Repta's hull. Max yanked at the steering lever, and flicked the turbos to full speed. The engines squealed. The pod shuddered, straining against the chain, but it was no use.

"Stuck, Max!" Rivet barked. The chain tugged on, pulling the pod towards Repta's open jaws, with Max and Rivet inside it. Through the watershield Max could see Repta's fiery eyes watching him. The robot's beak snapped wide open, a gaping black hole, surrounded by sharp metal teeth.

"Evacuate, Max!" Rivet barked. There was nothing else for it... Max grabbed Iris's capsule from the dashboard, hit the emergency escape, and took a deep breath. With a powerful jolt, his seat flipped forwards, firing him through an escape hatch in the floor. A moment later, he was shooting through the water alongside Rivet. He looked up to see Repta's beak close around the pod with a splintering crunch.

The robot shook its massive head, then opened its jaws, sending the pod spinning towards the seabed. It landed with a crash in

a sparking heap of bent and twisted metal.

Max tore his gaze from the wreck of his sub to see Repta swooping towards him, its eyes fixed on Iris's capsule. A Targonite spike shot from the Robobeast's side, opening into a claw as it zipped toward him. Max tightened his grip on Iris, kicked his legs, and dived out of the path of the claw. *No way! Not again!* The claw shot past him and ploughed into a hut. Max glanced back at Repta to see another claw already shooting out after him. He swerved right, feeling the current of the metal spike slicing past.

"Danger, Max!" Rivet barked. Max glanced back to see Repta's blaster cannons recoil and two bright balls of energy hurtle his way. Before he could move, his dogbot slammed into his shoulder, knocking him sideways. The fizzing energy balls whizzed past.

"Thanks, Riv!" Max shouted.

The energy spheres plunged on, smashing into a Merryn farm building with a boom, sending more stone bursting out. A huge chunk crashed into Rivet, knocking him sideways. The current of the blast hit Max, swirling him around. Sickening pain exploded in his elbow as a rock glanced off it. Iris's capsule shot from his numb fingers. *No!* Max dived after Iris but his dead arm slowed him down. The capsule spun away towards the chaos below. With a flick of his giant flippers, Repta powered through the water, yellow eyes locked on the capsule.

"Rivet fetch!" the dogbot barked, zooming towards the capsule, ears pricked.

Iris's hologram projected from her silver capsule, a manic grin plastered across her face as she watched Rivet speed towards her.

"Stop, Rivet!" Max cried. But it was too late. Rivet opened his mouth and snatched the capsule. Iris let out a victorious whoop and her hologram was sucked back into her capsule. Rivet's eyes flashed red. His body froze, and his jaws jerked open. Max's stomach clenched as he saw Iris's capsule fixed to Rivet's silicone tongue. Iris's voice echoed from Rivet's mouth. "This puny dogbot is mine!"

CHAPTER FOUR

TANKBOT TERROR

*O**h no, Rivet! What have you done?***

Rivet's propellers whirred as he raced to meet Repta. The vast robotic turtle plunged onwards, the path of the two robots making a V in the silty water as they came together. Max kicked his legs, following his dogbot, but he knew he'd never get to Rivet before Repta did.

"Don't worry, Max! I'm on it!" Lia called, shooting up from a cloud of clearing silt, and zooming towards Rivet from below. Max willed Lia and Spike on, but Rivet had a head start on them and he was swimming at full speed.

Just before Repta and Rivet collided, the dogbot levelled, swimming above Repta's head. Iris's capsule tumbled from the dogbot's jaws. Spike knifed towards it, and Lia reached out her hand, but Repta swiped its vast head sideways, butting the Merryn

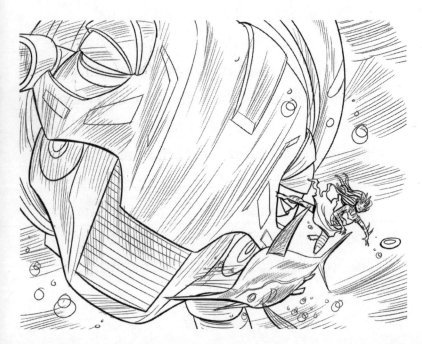

princess and her swordfish out of the way. Lia and Spike tumbled through the water. Max's stomach clenched as he saw Iris's silver capsule fuse to Repta's armoured head once more. Immediately, Repta's eyes lit up scarlet, casting long red beams through the water. The vast robot turned away from Max to face Fortress Prime and began to climb towards the green dome hovering over the fields. Its beak snapped open, and Iris's voice projected out.

"Come to me, my army!" her girlish voice sang. Max saw hundreds of round holes open in the metal platform at the base of Fortress Prime. The tankbots shot out, their legs and heads retracted inside their spiny metal shells so they flew like cannonballs through the water. Max gulped. *We have to save the village!* He searched the murky water for Lia and saw her scrambling back onto Spike, staring at the incoming missiles, her eyes wide with horror.

"Lia!" Max called. "Head down and organise a defence! I'll stop as many of those things as I can."

"Okay, Max!" Lia said, her face pale, but determined. Then she and Spike swam down into what was left of Astar.

Max spotted Rivet floating dazed in the water, his eyes dark and his robotic body still. "Wake up, Rivet!" Max called. Rivet's eyes flashed, and he shook himself, then powered towards Max, his metal tail between his legs.

"Sorry, Max!" Rivet barked. "Iris got Rivet!"

"Can't be helped, Riv!" Max said. "Now our job is to protect Astar from those tankbots!"

Rivet turned to face the huge swarm of approaching missiles and bared his teeth in a fearful grimace. "Got it, Max!" he barked.

Max glanced down to see Lia and Elra

hustling the Merryn farmers into lines, each man and woman equipped with a crystal-edged scythe or axe. Max turned back to the deadly hail of tankbots, almost on Astar, and felt sick. *If I don't stop those robots it's going to be carnage down there!* Repta was hanging in the water between Astar and Fortress Prime, its red eyes surveying the battleground.

As soon as the tankbots were in range, Max lifted his blaster and started to fire. He kept his finger on the trigger and scattered energy bolts through the ocean, hitting tankbot after tankbot with the beam. Each shot smashed a tankbot off course. Max kept on firing and firing, sending the tankbots flying off at all angles. Adrenaline pulsed through his veins. *This is working! I'm getting somewhere!* But then he noticed with a jolt that the tankbots he'd deflected were changing course, swerving back towards the

Merryn settlement, undamaged. He kept firing round after round but the tankbots powered on, gaining speed.

Max drew his hyperblade. A tankbot thundered towards him. Max swung and sliced at the cannonball, his blade biting deep into the metal. Max tugged his hyperblade free and he saw the tankbot's glowing eyes flicker out. *Yes!* The tankbot spun away at an angle and careered into a field, throwing up a plume of tattered seagrass. Max sliced at

another spiked metal orb as it shot past him, scoring a deep cut that sparked and smoked.

"Charge!" Elra cried below. Lia and Elra swooped upwards on their swordfish, with a dozen farmers on orcas at their backs. The Merryn let out a chorus of battle cries as they surged towards the approaching tankbots. Lia thrust her spear into one of them, sending it spinning away, trailing a plume of soot. Elra split another in two with her coral sword. The Merryn farmers shot off towards

targets of their own, crystal-edged weapons drawn back, teeth gritted. Battle cries and the sound of crystal on metal echoed all around.

"Take that!"

"Be gone, evil tech!"

Max hacked a tankbot in half, wincing as the impact jolted his arm. At his side, a young woman swung her axe, hacking a chunk off another.

"Ow!" The force sent her spinning backwards off her swordfish mount.

"Max! Coming at you!" Max heard Rivet bark. He turned to see the dogbot hurtling towards him, a tankbot on his tail. Max drew back his blade with two hands as Rivet shot past, then smashed his sword hard into the turtle's metal shell, with a satisfying crash. The sharp blade sliced straight through the metal, cutting the robot in half, exposing sizzling wires and glittering chips. *Yes!*

Rivet swerved back towards Max, and suddenly bared his metal teeth.

"Danger, Max!" the dogbot barked. "Bad turtles!" Something clamped hard around Max's sword arm, then sharp metal beaks grabbed both his ankles. Tankbots! They'd poked their heads and flippers from their shell and grabbed him from behind.

Max twisted and squirmed, but the robots' metal beaks just clamped tighter, making him gasp with pain. Rivet growled and snapped at the robots, but the powerful beaks held Max fast. More tankbots whizzed by on either side of Max, their slipstream tugging at his hair and clothes. One smashed into Rivet, sending him spinning away with a yelp.

Max gulped. He was trapped, his legs powerless in the turtles' beaks, a target out in the open. A red light shone into Max's eyes,

blinding him. He squinted into brightness
to see Repta flick its strong flipper-like legs
and power towards him, the red beams of its
eyes locked on him.

As it drew closer, Iris's voice blurted out
of the speakers on either side of its head.
"Max, there is no escape," she cried. "The
forces of Delta Quadrant are no match for

Fortress Prime! Join with us, or every one of you will be destroyed!"

CHAPTER FIVE

A SECOND DEADLY WAVE

Max squinted into the glare of Repta's evil red eyes, his heart thundering so hard he thought it might burst. He could see a glint of silver on top of the robot's head. *Iris's capsule.* The sight gave him a flash of hope. *It's Iris controlling that thing.* Max told himself. *I should be able to get through to her. She knows me. I reprogrammed her myself!* "Iris," Max cried, "you're not a killer! You need to fight the worm inside you. You're good – you were created to protect the people on board the SS *Liberty*." He paused for a moment, trying to see any flicker of change in the giant turtle before him but, if anything, the monster's eyes glowed brighter, a deeper blood-red than before.

From the village behind him came the boom of more explosions, and the clatter of falling stone. He could hear the battle cries of brave Merryn farmers alongside screams of terror and pain. Panic and hopelessness welled up inside him, tightening his chest and throat. "Iris!" he called again in desperation. "You can't hurt me. I'm your friend!"

For a heartbeat, he felt a glimmer of hope – Repta's eyes flickered from red to green. But then the green light faded and the red was back, brighter and bloodier still.

"I obey only General Zan," Iris shouted. "I will crush Astar and Aquora in the name of Fortress Prime." Repta's massive head shot

forwards, its long neck telescoping out. In the glare of the Robobeast's eyes, Max saw the monster's wide jaws swing open, surrounded by serrated teeth, powering towards him at the speed of a hover-train.

Boof! Something powerful and heavy smashed into Max's side from behind. His head snapped forwards and his teeth sank into his tongue with a searing pain as he was torn free of the tankbot's vice-like grip. Repta's snapping beak clanged shut beside him. Max turned to see fragments of shattered tankbot falling from the Robobeast's crunching jaws. Beside Max, tail wagging and tongue lolling, paddled Rivet. *He saved me!* Max realised.

"Okay, Max?" barked the dogbot. Max nodded, despite the throbbing bruises on his back where Rivet had hit him.

"Good boy!" Max said. "That's twice in one day you've saved me!" Max grabbed his dogbot's back. "Now, get us out of here!" Rivet shot off.

Max glanced back to see Repta spit the last fragments of tankbot from its beak, then turn to scan the village. Dented and sparking tankbots scattered the ground, and the Astarians were regrouping. Repta fixed its hungry stare on the ranks of villagers brandishing weapons. Sick dread welled in Max's belly at the sight.

"We've got to help them, boy," Max cried.

"We have to stop Repta."

Rivet swerved to a halt.

"Over here, Retpa!" Max cried. The robot's head snapped around. Max drew his blaster and gazed into the Robobeast's glaring red eyes, finger ready over the trigger.

Suddenly, the screech of whale song pierced the water. A team of at least twenty black-and-white orcas with Merryn farmers on their backs charged past Max. The orcas

butted into Repta's shell all at once, ramming the giant Robobeast. The force shoved the robot through the ocean, back towards Fortress Prime. The farmers on their orcas charged after the giant turtle, stabbing with their crystal-tipped tools, slashing at spikes and severing metal chains.

Not far off, Max saw Lia and Elra hacking down the last remaining tankbots, before gliding over. "Nice work!" Max said. Lia grinned.

"Good riddance!" Elra said, brandishing her sword at the retreating Repta. She turned to Max. "I'm so sorry that we doubted you." She gestured to Fortress Prime. "This evil is clearly nothing to do with Aquora."

"No," Max said. "But General Zan won't give up until he destroys Astar and steals its resources. Fortress Prime can always build more tankbots. No one is safe in the Delta

Quadrant if I can't fix Iris."

"But how?" Lia said. "She's attached to a war machine!" The blood drained from her face. "And it looks like Fortress Prime won't have to build more tankbots." Max followed her gaze, and felt a spike of piercing dread. The circular holes in the base of the floating city had opened. A second wave of tankbots – twice as many as in the first – shot out towards Astar.

"Retreat!" Elra called desperately to her farmers. She watched as their orcas turned and sped back towards the village, fleeing the barrage of tankbots, and the returning Robobeast.

"Spiky turtles, Max!" Rivet barked. Max looked down at his dogbot, and something finally clicked into place in his brain.

"Of course!" Max said, "Why didn't I think of it before? Lia – I've got an idea. There's no time to explain, but I'll need to get close to Iris for it to work. Can you help Elra and the villagers defend Astar from those tankbots? I'll deal with Repta."

"Okay," Lia said, "but you'd better be quick." Her eyes flicked to the tankbot wrecking balls hurtling towards them. "We won't be able to withstand that kind of bombardment for long."

Lia and Elra turned their swordfish, and sped back towards the village.

Max took hold of Rivet, and spun to face Repta. The giant turtle was hovering above the seagrass, watching its tankbot army whizzing towards Astar.

"Iris!" Max shouted. "You'll never succeed. You're nothing more than a computer programme with an over-inflated ego. I've beaten you before, and I'll beat you again!" Repta's long neck swept around and its red eyes locked on Max.

With a blast of static, General Zan's voice echoed through the water from Fortress Prime. "Kill that human boy!" he cried.

Repta shot towards Max and Rivet, mouth gaping and red eyes blazing with a furious light.

"Rivet!" Max said. "Head to the kelp fields. And charge up your electromagnetic pulse generators on the way. It's time to catch a turtle!"

CHAPTER SIX

WEAVING A WEB

Max gritted his teeth and held on to Rivet with all his strength as he was jolted and jerked through the water, tankbots careering past him on either side. Rivet dodged left and right, his thrusters roaring, and Max kicked his legs out behind them. *We have to get to the kelp fields before Repta catches us!* The red beams of Repta's furious gaze lit the ocean all around them, and Max could hear the throb of the Robobeast's motors right behind. He glanced over his shoulder and his mouth went dry – the robotic turtle's sharp beak was inching towards him, gaining steadily.

Zap! Zap! Bright flashes of energy blasted from Repta's cannons and seared through the water towards him. "Up, Rivet!" Max cried. The dogbot climbed sharply and Max pulled his legs towards his chest. The sizzling energy blasts fizzed past beneath his feet.

The huge dome of Fortress Prime loomed ahead. Rivet dived, hurtling beneath the black Targonite base of the city, plunging Max into shadow. Max glanced up, but all he could see was smooth, dark metal, lit by the sullen glow of Repta's eyes behind them. A moment later they were back out in the open ocean, speeding over the seagrass towards the kelp tree line in the distance.

"EMP charged, Max!" Rivet barked.

"Get under cover as soon as we reach the kelp!" Max said. Rivet angled downwards, powering towards the tree line. Max glanced back and gulped. Repta was right at his heels. Ahead the tangled trunks of the flowering kelp filled his view, a thick web of twisted green, with dark shadow beyond.

"You can't escape me!" Iris shrieked.

"If you want to catch me, you'll have to find me first!" Max yelled back, just as Rivet tugged him between a pair of winding trunks and into the forest of kelp.

"Keep going, boy!" Max said. Rivet slalomed between branches, pulling Max with him further into the tangled darkness of the forest.

BOOM! A strong current hit them from behind, and the thick, black silt of thousands of years of rotting vegetation swirled around them. *Repta fired into the forest!* Max glanced back, but all he could see was dark, murky water between the winding branches and trunks. *Ha! Iris has made it even harder to find us!* As if in answer to his thoughts, Max heard a screech of frustration echo around him from Repta's speakers.

"Riv, stop here," Max said. "I'm going to programme an electromagnetic pulse that should put an end to that worm." Rivet paddled to a stop, and Max flicked the panel in his side, revealing the dogbot's programming touch screen. Another muffled boom shook

the forest, sending a rain of bright petals fluttering down around Max and Rivet. Rivet let out a whimper as the forest around them shook.

"Don't worry, Riv," Max said, tapping away at the dogbot's programming interface, working in the faint green glow from its screen. "Iris won't find us down here. Not until we want her to." *Or, at least, that's the plan...* Max flicked Rivet's side compartment closed. "All done," he said. "Now, you stay hidden until I call. I'm going to get Repta. We'll need to get close to Iris for your EMP to work."

"Okay, Max!" Rivet barked, his red eyes glowing bright in the gloom. Max took off through the winding trunks, dodging shadowy branches in the silty water until he noticed a faint red glow all around him. He kicked upwards, brushing through the flowers of the tree canopy, and peered out over the top.

Repta hovered above, scanning the gloomy forest.

"Over here!" Max shouted. Repta's neck snaked round and its gaze locked on Max.

"Foolish boy! You will die," Iris cried, and Repta's head shot down towards Max. Max dived back through the flowers and branches. *Crash!* Repta's head plunged through the kelp behind him. Max looked back to see the turtle's vast domed head bending the stems, straining onwards, mouth opening and shutting, but the kelp was too strong and too dense.

"You can't reach me!" Max called up. Repta's red eyes flashed. A thick spike shot down through the canopy, slicing towards Max. Max leapt sideways, his skin tingling and his heart skipping as the current from the spike brushed his ear.

Thunk! The spike sank deep into a thick, woody kelp trunk. Max darted away, pushing through snaggling twigs, past the barbed spike. Looking back, Max saw the grappling chain pulled taut as Repta tried to tug the spike free.

"You missed, Iris!" Max shouted up at Repta. He positioned himself in front of a thick clump of tangled branches and looked up through the tree canopy, catching a glimpse of Repta's red-eyed stare, peering back at him through the kelp. Another grappling spike zipped through the canopy, and Max dived aside. *Crash!* The spike tangled around the trunks, sticking fast.

"You can't keep dodging me! I'm going to skewer you alive!" Iris shrieked. Max swam a short distance, stopping when he reached a small clearing in the trees.

"I'm here!" he called up at Repta. A pair of Targonite metal points shot towards him, one from either side, and he dived into a roll. *Thud! Thunk!* Both spikes sank deep into woody trunks and lodged there. The kelp

creaked and shuddered as Iris tried to wind back Repta's spikes, but the ancient plants were rooted too deep, and the woody flesh was tough and strong.

"Rivet!" Max called to his dogbot. "I need you!" Max heard Rivet's propellers whir and before long, the dogbot's red eyes appeared in the shadows. *Crash!* One of Repta's hooks shook the canopy above, sending more flowers fluttering down. The whole forest trembled as if caught in a wild storm as Repta raged above the canopy, trying to pull itself free.

"Time to head up," Max told Rivet. Together, they swam through the winding branches and falling blossoms, out into the open water behind Repta. The giant turtle was bucking and straining against its chains lodged in the forest below, wrenching at the kelp. But it was caught like a fly in a web. Max and Rivet swam up over the turtle's shell to where Iris's silver capsule shimmered on the back of its head.

"Riv," Max said, "scan Iris for the worm. Then fire your electromagnetic pulse at it."

"Got it, Max," Rivet barked. His eyes flashed steadily as he focussed on Iris's capsule.

"You will never succeed!" Iris shouted. "Even if you destroy me, Fortress Prime will prevail. All hail, General Zan!"

"Found it, Max!" Rivet barked.

"Then fire," Max said. "But only target the worm. We don't want to damage Iris!"

"Okay, Max!" Rivet barked. He leaned in close to the capsule, almost touching it with the tip of his metal nose, then opened his jaws and let out what looked like a silent bark. Then Rivet drew back his muzzle.

"Done, Max!" he barked. Repta instantly stopped struggling. Its red eyes flickered, then turned green. Iris's face projected up from her capsule, the same bright green, and smiling with relief.

"That's better!" she said. "What a horrible experience. Even worse than being mad. I never want to be part of a killer turtle ever again! Thank you so much, Max and Rivet."

"Am I glad to see you back to your old self, Iris!" Max said. "Can you stop the tankbot army?"

"Already done, Max!" Iris said, and Max realised that he could no longer hear the crunch and crash of shattering stone drifting on the current from Astar.

A blast of static broke the quiet. "Attack!" General Zan's furious voice shouted. "Iris! What are you doing? Make my tankbots attack this instant!"

Iris flashed Max a wicked grin. "Do you think we should do as he asks?" Max felt a pang of worry, but Iris's face was still green, her eyes twinkling merrily. Suddenly, Max realised what she meant. He grinned too.

"Why not?" Max said. "I think it's time he got a taste of his own medicine. But don't destroy the city. There are too many people inside. Just focus on its defences." Gazing out over the tree canopy, Max could just make out the green dome of Fortress Prime. As he watched, tankbots hurtled towards the structure, slamming into the curved shield and sending bright green haloes of light rippling across its glassy surface.

"What's going on?" the general's voice shouted through the city's speakers, and Max could hear the boom of heavy objects falling through the static. "Tankbots, stop!" the general cried, as a great shower of them bombarded the dome. "Desist! Fire the other way!" Finally, the vast floating dome started to move, slowly at first, but gathering speed, sailing over the seagrass away from Astar, towards the kelp forest. A barrage of tankbots zoomed after it. Max and Rivet crouched low on Repta's back as the domed city, trailed by its tankbot entourage, whirred overhead and away, finally fading into the distant blue shadows of the ocean.

CHAPTER SEVEN

REPARATIONS

A few days later, Max steered his repaired pod over the kelp forest, Elra at his side. Ahead, the bulky metal form of Repta towered over the bright flowers and twisting branches of the forest, frozen, silent and dull-eyed. "So, what do you think?" Max asked.

Elra ran her gaze over the colossal robot and smiled. "I think it works. An excellent scarefish – no pests will try to eat the harvest with that thing frightening them off."

"You don't think it looks…out of place?"

Lia asked, frowning up at the statue from Spike's back.

"No," Elra said. "It will remind us of Simon and what can happen to someone if you isolate them, just for being different. Maybe if we'd been kinder, like you said, he would never have started experimenting on himself with robotics, and resorted to creating his monstrosities. A robot of our own will remind us to be tolerant of strangers."

"Okay," Lia said. "I guess that makes sense." But she didn't sound convinced.

"Well, I think it looks elegant," Iris piped up from the dashboard.

"And it's quite safe, now I've removed all its wires to repair the sub," Max added. "Fortress Prime can't ever use it against Astar again."

"No." Elra nodded slowly, her face suddenly grave. "We have you to thank for saving us from that threat. But I have a feeling we haven't seen the last of General Zan and his people."

"Well, if they come back, you can count on Aquora's aid, as well as Sumara's," Max said. "Aquorans used to be fearful of Merryn, too, before we met Lia. Now we work together to defend Nemos from danger." Max turned to Lia. "We'd better get going," he said. "We're going to have to issue a full report to my father about General Zan."

Lia nodded. "Goodbye, Elra," she said. "I'll look forward to seeing you when you're next in Sumara."

"You too!" Elra said. "And you can be sure the next time you visit Astar, you will be greeted very differently."

Max and Lia turned away from the statue-like form of Repta and set off over the flowering kelp.

"So, what do you think of the flowering kelp now?" Lia asked.

"It is pretty amazing," Max said, gazing through his watershield at the fluttering flowers. "And it saved our lives. It's been here longer than humans, and can even withstand a Robobeast attack. I've got a feeling it will still be here long after Aquora is gone from Nemos."

Lia shot Max a puzzled look through the

watershield. "I think that bump on the head might have addled your brains," she said. "You hardly sound like a tech geek at all."

They passed over the last of the flowering kelp and into the seagrass fields. Below, Max could see the Merryn farmers working with their swordfish and orcas, repairing craters and collecting fallen stones.

"The village looks almost back to normal!" Max said. Most of the dwellings had been repaired while he was working on the pod and Repta – not to mention the fiddly task of picking the control worm out of Iris's capsule.

"Apart from that massive pile of metal turtles," Lia said, pointing at the mound of deactivated tankbots lying at the edge of the final seagrass field.

"My father will collect them soon enough," Max said. "We'll need to run tests on them to learn more about the technology of Fortress Prime. Elra is right. General Zan will be back. But Aquora and Sumara will be ready." Max eased himself back in his seat and let out a yawn. "Iris, take us back to Aquora." He glanced at her smiling green face before closing his eyes. "I'm going to take a nap. I've

seen enough nature to last me a lifetime!"
"Of course, Max. Next stop – Aquora."

THE END

Don't miss the next Sea Quest book,
in which Max faces

GORT
THE DEADLY SNATCHER

Read on for a sneak preview!

CHAPTER ONE

PEACE

Max's stomach fizzed with excitement as he swam through clear waters, making one final check on his father's latest construction. It was a giant, air-filled plexiglass dome, right at the heart of the Merryn city of Sumara. Max ran his eyes slowly over each hexagonal panel, looking for cracks, or the slightest trickle of bubbles. Through the plexiglass, he could see black-clad Aquoran technicians scurrying about like insects inside the dome.

"No holes, Max!" Rivet, Max's dogbot barked from just ahead.

"Just as well!" Lia said. The Merryn princess frowned at the giant structure from the back of her swordfish, Spike. "I can't believe our guests are about to arrive and we're still checking for leaks!"

Max grinned. "Dad's just being extra cautious. We've been all over the dome a hundred times. And it's made using the latest tech!"

"Hmm," Lia said, "maybe that's what's worrying me." Then she smiled. "Anyway, I can't wait for the ceremony to start!" Max felt a swell of pride as ran his eyes over the dome. Without his father's technical skills, Sumara's first deep-sea peace conference would never have been possible.

The sound of chatter and laughter drifted up to them along with the salty tang of seaweed cakes and festive treats.

Max turned away from the dome and gazed down over Sumara's broad main street, Treaty Avenue. The wide street ran from Treaty Square, straight through the

dome, then out the other side, and on to Lia's father's palace. Glowing spheres mounted on coral pillars bathed the avenue in silver light. Merryn of all ages lined the approach to the dome, pressed tightly together, wearing their best beaded tunics. Max could see children and babies on their parents' shoulders waving bright flags.

"It looks like everyone in Sumara's turned

out to greet their guests!" Max said.

Lia nodded. "And we couldn't have hoped for better weather." The current stirred her long silver hair, making it shimmer in the soft glow filtering from the dome. The water was crystal clear, with no silt to muddy the view of the surrounding coral towers of Sumara.

"True," Max said. "Which means they should be on time." He lifted his eyes to scan the ocean beyond the city. "In fact – I think that's the first of them arriving now!"

A narrow submarine barge, faceted to shine like a diamond, was gliding slowly towards Sumara, reflecting the lights and colours of the underwater city.

"Pretty boat, Max!" Rivet barked. A chorus of cheers went up from the crowd as the gleaming barge reached Treaty Avenue, then inched towards the docks on the side of the dome.

DISCOVER THE FIRST SERIES
OF SEA QUEST:

978 1 40831 848 5   978 1 40831 849 2   978 1 40831 850 8   978 1 40831 851 5

DON'T MISS THE NEXT SPECIAL BUMPER BOOK:

HYDROR
THE OCEAN HUNTER!

978 1 40834 097 4

www.seaquestbooks.co.uk

WIN AN EXCLUSIVE
GOODY BAG

In every Sea Quest book the Sea Quest logo is
hidden in one of the pictures. Find the logo in this book,
make a note of which page it appears on and
go online to enter the competition at

www.seaquestbooks.co.uk

We will be picking five lucky winners to win
some special Sea Quest goodies.

You can also send your entry on a postcard to:

Sea Quest Competition,
Orchard Books, Carmelite House
50 Victoria Embankment
London EC4Y 0DZ

Don't forget to include your name and address!

GOOD LUCK

Closing Date: 31st August 2016

IF YOU LIKE SEA QUEST, YOU'LL LOVE BEAST QUEST!

Series 1: COLLECT THEM ALL!

An evil wizard has enchanted the magical Beasts of Avantia. Only a true hero can free the Beasts and save the land. Is Tom the hero Avantia has been waiting for?

FERNO
THE FIRE DRAGON

978 1 84616 483 5

SEPRON
THE SEA SERPENT

978 1 84616 482 8

ARCTA
THE MOUNTAIN GIANT

978 1 84616 484 2

TAGUS
THE HORSE MAN

978 1 84616 486 6

NANOOK
THE SNOW MONSTER

978 1 84616 485 9

EPOS
THE FLAME BIRD

978 1 84616 487 3